this book belongs to

....

Ingredients

For K&E – A.L.
For Jon – L.B.

PICTURE CORGI

UK | USA | Canada | Ireland | Australia
India | New Zealand | South Africa
Picture Corgi is part of the Penguin Random House group of companies
whose addresses can be found at global.penguinrandomhouse.com.
www.penguin.co.uk   www.puffin.co.uk   www.ladybird.co.uk

Penguin
Random House
UK

First published 2016
001

Printed in China
A CIP catalogue record for this book is available from the British Library

ISBN: 978–0–552–57518–8
All correspondence to:
Picture Corgi, Penguin Random House Children's,
80 Strand, London WC2R 0RL

FSC
MIX
Paper from
responsible sources
FSC® C018179

Thanks, Kittie, Beast x

Love, Bella ♡

The Fairytale Hairdresser

and the

PRINCESS AND THE PEA

Abie Longstaff
&
Lauren Beard

PICTURE CORGI

Kittie Lacey was the best hairdresser in all the land.

This summer her salon was very popular.
The Queen was hosting a food festival to find
her son a princess, and everyone wanted a
special foodie hairstyle.

Snow White chose to celebrate her favourite fruit – apples.

Red Riding Hood asked for curls like strawberries.

And Mr Gingerbread Man wanted his icing quiff shaped like a banana.

That night there was a terrible storm. Through the pouring rain, Kittie heard
the doorbell ring. On the step stood a girl.
"I'm Penelope," said the girl.
"Come in!" cried Kittie. "You can stay here till the storm passes."

Penelope was a chef and she told Kittie about her plans to travel the world,
cooking all kinds of food.

The next morning Prince Peter came to the salon to have his hair done.
He looked very worried.

"The palace chef is ill!" he told Kittie. "He can't cook for the festival and we
don't know what to do. Mum is so upset. She's invited princesses from all over
the land to meet me. What will everyone eat?"

"I know someone who can help," said Kittie, and she introduced
Prince Peter to Penelope.
"I'd love to cook for the festival!" Penelope cried.
"Oh, thank you," said the prince.

They all went to the palace together.
Peter showed Kittie and Penelope
his garden full of vegetables.
There was a huge pumpkin,

a little nut tree with a silver nutmeg
and a golden pear,

and a turnip so enormous it took
Peter, Kittie and Penelope to pull
it out of the ground.

Peter and Penelope chatted non-stop about food and recipes and table settings.

Kittie left her friends gazing into each other's eyes and headed for the Royal Powder Room, where the Queen wanted her help styling the visiting princesses.

To Kittie's surprise, the styling chair was set up a little strangely. The Queen was very excited. "When Peter was born, the fairies gave me a magic pea!" she said. "It's a secret test to find the right girl."

She showed Kittie the instructions.

How to find the perfect

step 1 You will need:

• Prince Peter's magic pea
• Lots of cushions

step 2 Place the cushions on a chair and place the pea under the cushions

person for Prince Peter

Step 3) Person must sit on chair

Feels comfortable?
Not the right Person

Feels uncomfortable?
You've found the right
person

ouch!

×

✓

Congratulations

"I just know the right girl will be a princess!" said the Queen.

But Kittie wasn't so sure.

Meanwhile a witch was hatching an evil plan.
"I want to marry the prince," she cried, and she waved her wand.

In an instant, she was transformed into a beautiful princess.

The witch joined the queue of girls waiting to have their hair done.

In the Royal Powder Room, Kittie styled princess after princess.

"Are you comfortable, dear?" asked the Queen, every time a new princess sat on the cushions.

"Oh, yes, thank you!" each one replied.
The Queen looked more and more disappointed.

Kittie worked all day long. And so did Penelope.

By the end of the day, there was only one princess left to style.
"Oh, Kittie," said the Queen. "None of the princesses has noticed the pea!
This is the last princess in the land. She *has* to be the right girl!"

The final princess sat down on the chair . . .

"Ah," she sighed daintily. "These cushions are so lovely and soft."
The Queen burst into tears. "Then *you* can't marry the prince either!"
"WHAT?" cried the princess. She was furious.
"You didn't pass the test," the Queen explained. "You didn't feel the pea under the cushion."

The princess was so angry! Before Kittie's eyes she transformed into a witch!
The witch snatched the pea from under the cushion.
"If I can't marry the prince," she cackled, "then no one can!"

Kittie looked around. What could she do? Suddenly she had an idea . . .

Kittie gave the styling chair
a hard spin.
Round and round went the
witch until she was dizzy.

"Guards!" called the Queen. "Seize her!"

The witch was marched off to jail.

"Oh, what shall I do?" cried the Queen. "Not one of the princesses was right."

"There is one person you haven't tried yet," replied Kittie and she put the pea back under the cushion.

Just then, Peter and Penelope came into the Royal Powder Room.
Penelope was exhausted! She slumped onto the styling chair.
"Ow!" she cried as she jumped off again. "That cushion is really lumpy."
The Queen gasped. "Penelope is the right girl for my son!" she declared.

"I didn't need a test to know that!" Peter said, looking into Penelope's eyes. Penelope smiled and took his hand. "Let's go to the festival together," she said.

Kittie helped Peter and Penelope try on outfits for the food festival.

Soon they found
something just right . . .

And the happy couple danced all night in the moonlight.

Before long they were married, and after a wonderful wedding Prince Peter and Princess Penelope showed Kittie their honeymoon plans to travel around the world.

"Thank you, Kittie," they cried as they waved goodbye to their friend
Kittie Lacey, the best hairdresser in all the land.